IZZIE

IZZIE

by Susan Pearson

paintings by
Robert Andrew Parker

The Dial Press · New York

Library of Congress Cataloging in Publication Data
Pearson, Susan. Izzie.
[1. Dolls—Fiction] I. Parker, Robert Andrew, ill. II. Title.
PZ7.P323316Iz [Fic] 74-18597
ISBN 0-8037-4904-X   ISBN 0-8037-4905-8 lib. bdg.

To Gerry Turkel,
for his tolerance of giraffes

Cary was three and a half the night her father brought his friend Izzie home for dinner. She hadn't met Izzie before, but he brought her a cloth cat-doll. It had a white painted-on face and a white body, and its legs and arms and ears were blue-and-white stripes. Cary named him Izzie too, and he had his first dinner by candlelight that same night.

That summer Cary's mother taught nature at a fancy day camp. The nature cabin was small, with lots of windows and a big stone fireplace. On rainy days the campers sat on the floor and listened to six records of different birds' sounds. When it was sunny again, they all walked very quietly through the woods, listening for real birds.

The camp also had a craft shop, a lake with a diving raft, and a stable. Cary loved the horses best. Izzie got stepped on by a pony once, but they sewed his tummy up fine in the craft shop. One of the campers said, "He looks like he had his appendix out."

To Cary, August meant Maine and Uncle Morris and Aunt Doris. Cary liked everything about them: where they lived, how their names rhymed, and especially their lobster afternoons. Then Cary and her four cousins all piled into the back of the clunky old pick-up truck, Uncle Morris climbed into the driver's seat, and they were off for the ocean.

There they walked far out on a long pier. At the end of it a lobster man was sitting on a bench in the sun outside his shack. Grinning, he got up and pulled three crates out of the water, and there inside, crawling over each other, were the shiny wet lobsters. They each picked out their own.

"How about one for the hungry cat there?" said the lobster man. So they took one more for Izzie and good measure.

When they got home, Aunt Doris dropped the lobsters, one by one, into a pot of boiling water. When they turned red, they were done.

Then everyone sat down at two picnic tables pushed together under the maple tree, pulling the meat from the hard shells and dipping each piece into a bowl of melted butter. When you cracked the shells open, juice sprayed all over, and everyone ended up with a face full of butter and lobster juice. It was a slurpy, sloppy, happy meal, and Izzie enjoyed it as much as Cary. Most of his juice and butter stains came out in the next day's laundry.

In the early fall the grapes were ripe. The arbor in the very back of their yard didn't look so big, but there were plenty of grapes. Dad and Cary sang "Sadie" and "She'll be Comin' Round the Mountain" while they picked, and every so often they sat on the ground and ate some of the pickings. When Mother said, "There won't be enough for any jam if you two keep eating them all," they got up and picked again.

When they had picked the last grape, Cary sat Izzie in the only half-full bucket and they walked back to the house. Inside, Dad washed all the grapes and Mother put them in a kettle on the stove. Then they sat at the kitchen table and ate the leftovers while the warm grape smell filled the room.

"I'll bet Izzie's the only purple-fannyed cat within thirty miles," Dad said. "Goes well with his appendectomy."

Johnny Sperber's yard had the most and the biggest trees. It took Mr. Sperber the whole last two weeks of October to rake all the leaves into the street for the garbage men to pick up. One Saturday Johnny and Cary helped. By seven thirty that night the street pile was enormous. Cary and Johnny put their rakes in the shed, raced back to the pile, and jumped into it. Just before Cary jumped in, she threw Izzie in too.

The leaves were soft and made a crackling sound. You could bury yourself in them and still breathe, but you got dust in your eyes if you kept them open. They jumped into the pile some more, and then lay down on top of it and threw leaves into the air, watching them float back down.

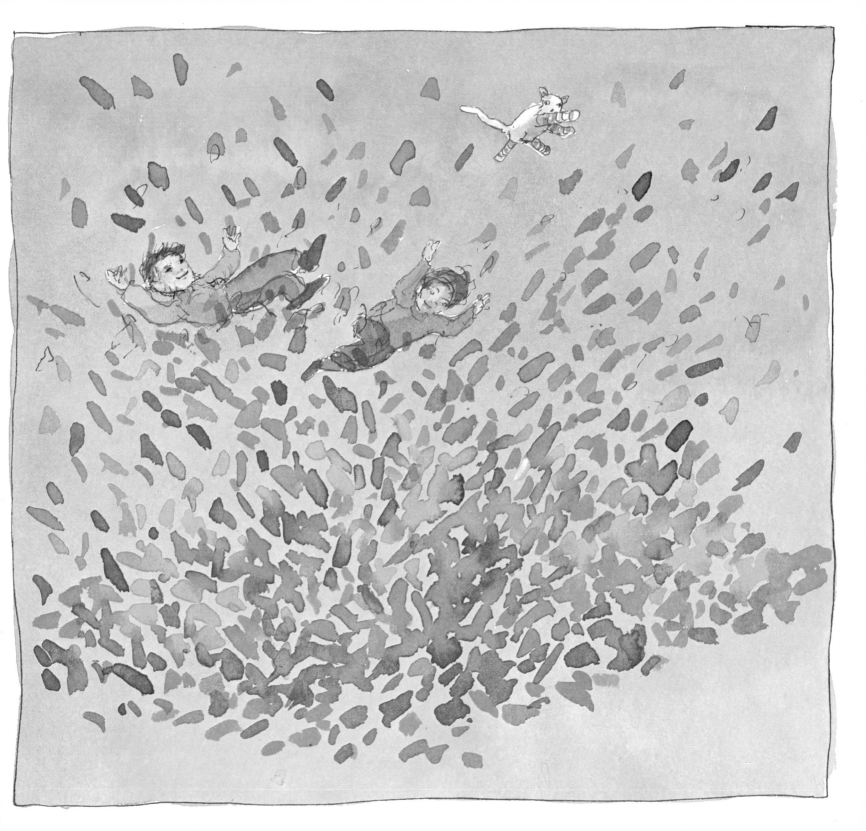

Afterward Cary took Izzie home with a torn right foot. They never could figure out just how that happened, but Mother sewed a patch on it in the morning. The patch was red-and-white polka dot, and it looked shiny and new on Izzie's faded blue-and-white striped leg.

Three weeks before Christmas, Mother started baking for the holidays. Best of all the preparations, Cary thought, was the Julbrod. Mother mixed up the dough, put it in a big greasy bowl, and covered the bowl with a dishcloth. In an hour it had grown into twice as much. When Cary punched it down it made a hissing sound and then it was back to the same size they started with. Next they pushed raisins and nuts and candied fruits into it. After it had risen a second time and been punched down again, they divided the dough into nine pieces. They rolled out each piece as if they were making clay snakes, then braided three of the snakes together and shaped each braid into a wreath. They let the three loaves rise for half an hour before putting them into the oven.

The kitchen was steamy with the smell of bread and Christmas, and the windows were all fogged up from the heat of the oven. When the bread was done, Cary and Mother were covered with flour and Izzie was sticky with dough, but the Julbrod was truly beautiful.

Cary's birthday was really the day before Christmas, but because everyone was away visiting then, her birthday party was December 16. Johnny Sperber and Maggie Shamamian and Heather Ryan and Gerry Fogelman were all coming.

The dining-room table was covered with holly, and above it Mother had hung all colors and sizes and shapes of balloons. After lunch and the cake, which was shaped like a clown and had four candles plus one to grow on, the five of them and Izzie went sledding on LaSalle Hill.

It had snowed again the night before, and the new snow sprayed in your face as you slid down the hill. When the streetlights came on and the gray sky made the snow look even whiter, it was time to go home. Mother had made a fire in the fireplace and there was hot chocolate ready.

Later, when everyone had left, Izzie was still cold and wet from the snowy afternoon. They put him in the drier, and when Cary took him to bed he was warm and toasty next to the cold sheets.

Spring came late that year, and when it did it rained for eight days straight. On the ninth day the dirt behind the garage was a glorious mud-pile. On the tenth day, the mud was just right for pies.

Cary filled heart-shaped cake pans and fish-shaped jello molds while Izzie watched and tasted the batter. Then she decorated everything with new leaves and red berries from the bushes. While they were drying in the sun, she filled a cookie sheet with berry-chip cookies. Then she built a mud castle.

When Cary came into the kitchen, Mother said, "Into the tub with you!" Izzie went into the washing machine. When he came out, his polka-dot patch was beginning to look just as faded as the rest of him.

At the beginning of May Dad stood on the sidewalk and looked at their house. "This place looks awful," he said. "Time we painted."

Grampie Horsman came to help out. Dad painted the top of the house, Mother painted the middle, and Cary and Grampie painted the bottom. It was wonderful watching the dirty gray house turn white again. They painted all the shutters green before Dad put them back up, and the slats in the shutters made the paint splatter from the brush. Cary's green freckles came off with turpentine, but Izzie's didn't.

"That cat is turning into a regular rainbow," Grampie said. "A blue-and-white striped, red polka-dotted, purple splotched, green freckled rainbow."

By the time Cary was four and a half, Izzie was a year old. He looked about eighty-seven. His stuffing had been sewn back in seven times. His happy painted-on face was covered with green freckles. And you could almost see right through his stripes—and even his polka dots—they were so faded from his many washings. There was no doubt about it—everything about him was special.

One summer afternoon the woman next door came over. Her name was Esther and she was an artist. "I've got an idea," Mother said. "Let's fix Izzie up like new!"

She went to her sewing box and found some blue-and-white striped cotton and some plain white muslin. Then she set up the sewing machine, and she and Esther cut the cloth into pieces just like Izzie's pieces only a little bigger. Esther ran home for her paints. When she came back, she painted a face, exactly the same as Izzie's face, on the clean new material. Then they carefully sewed the pieces together, and inside the new Izzie they put the old Izzie. He looked like a new person, they all agreed.

That fall Cary started school. Lincoln Elementary School was six blocks from her house, and after the first day Cary went alone or with Johnny Sperber. The new Izzie just sat at home on her bed.

One October afternoon they had passed three piles of leaves on their way home. When Cary saw the fourth pile up ahead, she said, "I'll race you!"

They tore down the street together, straight to the pile, up into the air, and down, down into the soft crackling leaves.

"When is your dad going to start raking?" Cary asked as they got up and brushed themselves off.

"Saturday," Johnny answered. "Want to help?"

"Sure."

"Going to bring that old cat of yours?" he asked.

"Oh—he's not old anymore," Cary answered, and she told him about the new Izzie. "He's too clean to carry around now. He'd just get dirty again. Besides," she said, "I'm in school now."

"You know," said Johnny, "I'll sorta miss him."

"Me too," said Cary.

Susan Pearson

was born in Massachusetts, but spent many of her growing-up years in Minnesota. She has been writing stories since she was in the fifth grade. Now she lives in New York City, where she is a children's book editor.

Ms. Pearson really did have a ragdoll cat named Izzie. In fact, she still has it.

Robert Andrew Parker

is the well-known illustrator of many books, including *Pop Corn and Ma Goodness*, a 1970 Caldecott Medal runner-up; *The Trees Stand Shining*, selected by *School Library Journal* as one of the Best Books for Spring 1971 and an ALA Notable Book; and *Zeek Silver Moon*, one of *The New York Times* Outstanding Books of the Year, 1972.

Mr. Parker is the father of five sons, four of whom are professional drummers. At various times he has also played drums professionally. He lives in Carmel, New York.